10
Minute Tales

Guess with
jess

Chloe the Caterpillar

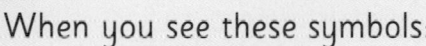

When you see these symbols:

Read aloud

Read aloud to
your child.

Read alone

Support your child
as they read alone.

Read along

Read along with
your child.

EGMONT

We bring stories to life

Read aloud   Read along

It's a sunny day on Greendale Farm.
Jess is going to find his new friend, Chloe.
Would you like to meet her? Come on!

"Hello, Willow," says Jess. "I've got a surprise
for you. You're going to meet my friend, Chloe!"

"Great! What kind of animal is she?" asks Willow.

"Why don't you guess what animal Chloe is while
I find her," says Jess, excitedly. "Bye, Willow!"

"Bye, Jess!" says Willow.

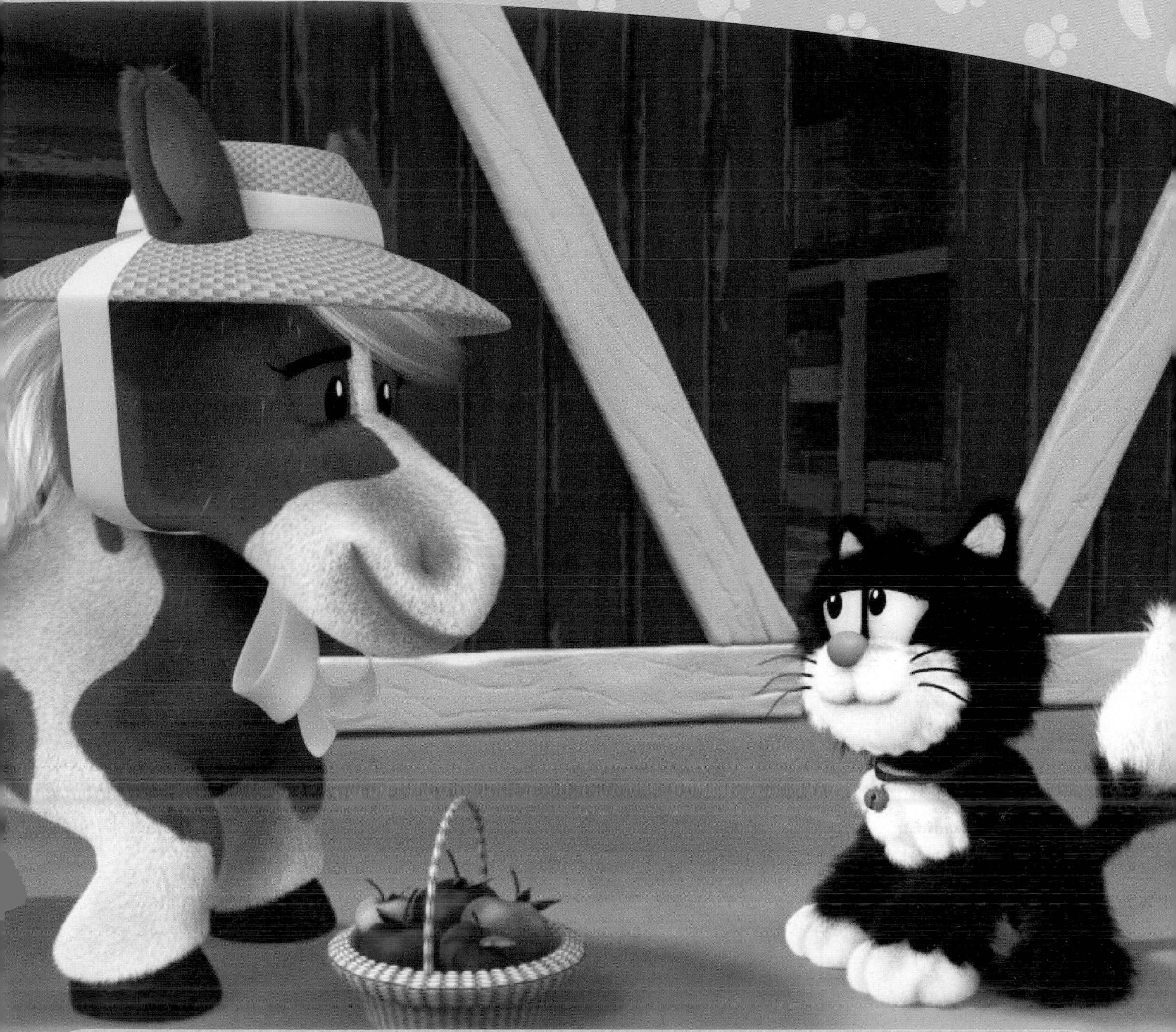

Jess is going to introduce Willow to his new friend, Chloe.

Would you like to know what Chloe is?

"She's small and black with a yellow line down her side and little hairy spikes all over her," says Jess.

What animal do you think she is?

"She's a caterpillar!" says Jess. "And she likes to eat lots of leaves, especially the leaves at Horace's pond. Will you help me find her? Come on!"

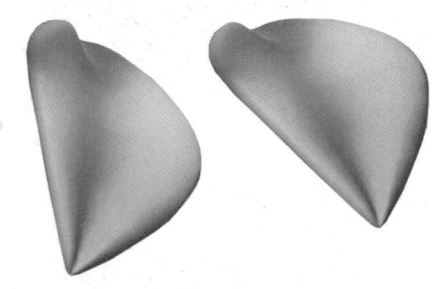

Read alone

Chloe is a caterpillar! Jess goes to look for her at the pond.

Read aloud   Read along

At the pond, Horace is sat on his lily pad playing his drum.

"Hey, Jess!" he says. "What are you doing?"

"Hello, Horace. I've come to see Chloe," says Jess and he goes to the blackcurrant bush.

But Jess can't find Chloe on the leaves.

"It's not like her to miss lunch," says Jess. "What's happened to Chloe the caterpillar?"

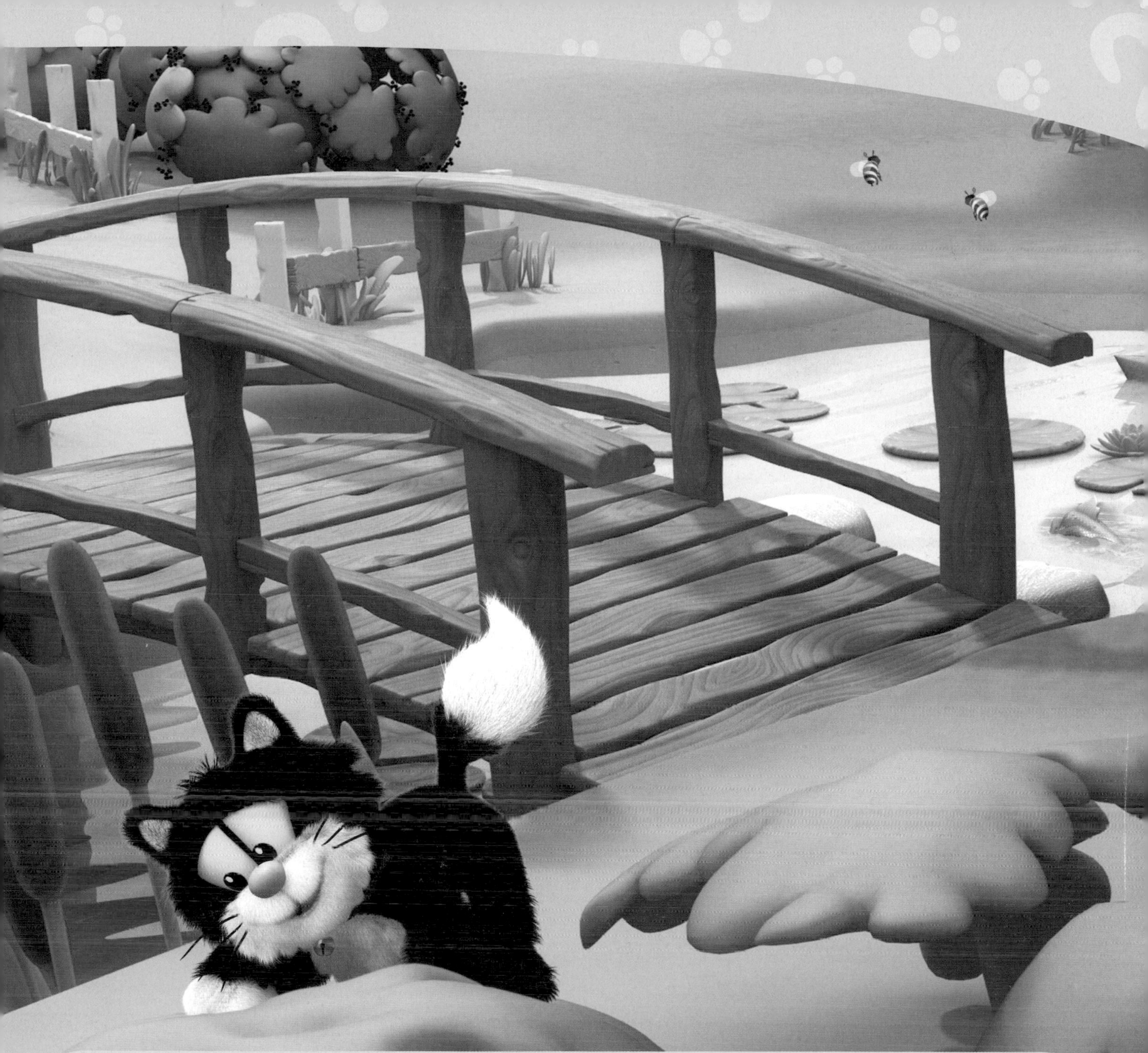

Jess can't find Chloe on the leaves by the pond.

Read aloud   Read along

Horace thinks that Chloe might have gone to find more leaves, so Jess goes to look for her on the Twisty Tree.

"Come on," says Jess. "Let's find Chloe!"

Joey and Jinx are chasing around the tree.

"Hello, Joey and Jinx. Will you help me look for Chloe the caterpillar?" asks Jess. "I think she might be on the Twisty Tree."

"Yeah! We'll help!" say Joey and Jinx, excitedly.

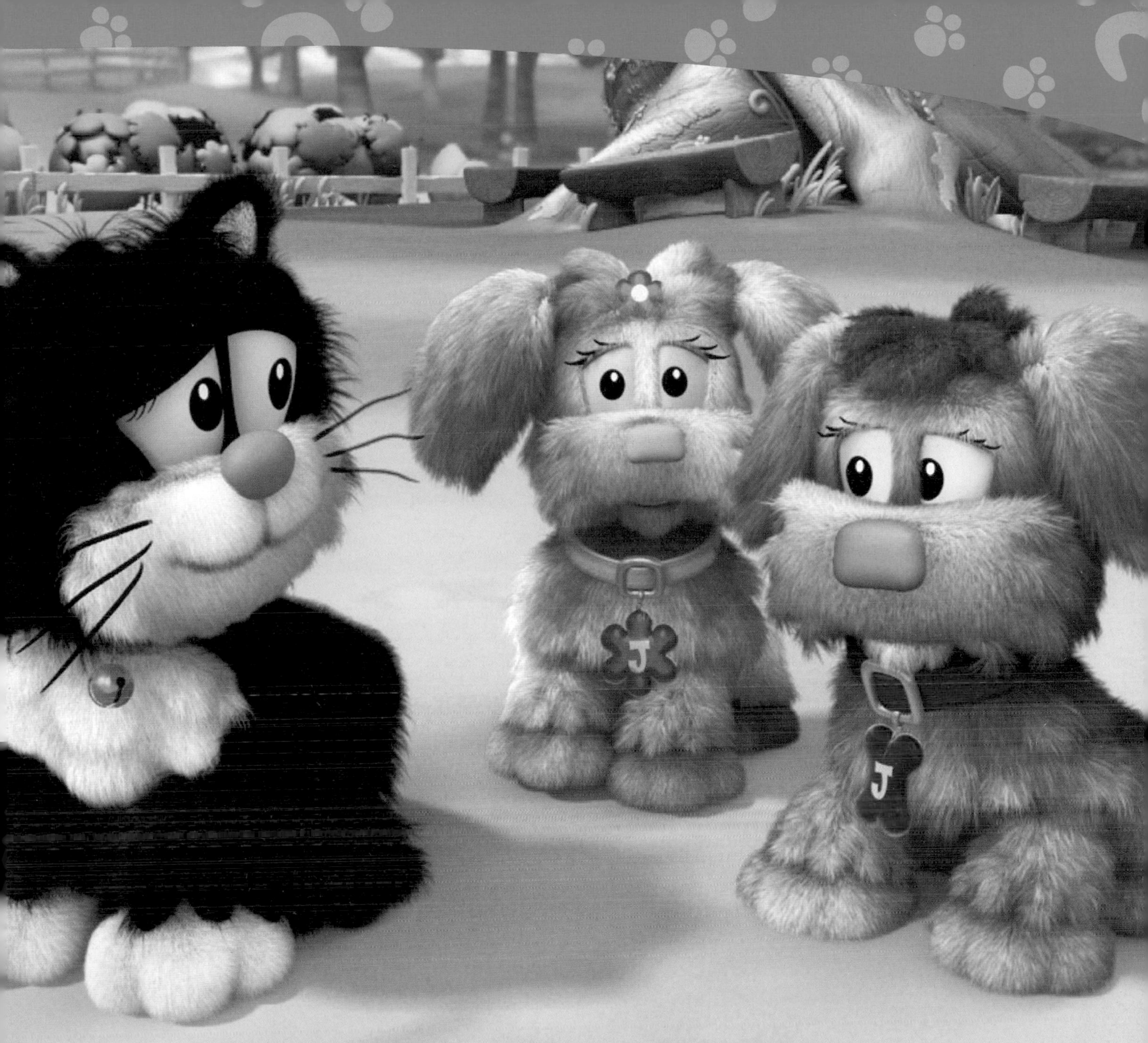

Jess goes to look for Chloe on the Twisty Tree. The puppies will help.

Read aloud Read along

Joey and Jinx jump up at the tree shouting, "Chloe! Furry-wurry caterpillar! Where are you?"

"Shhhh!" says Jess.

But Joey and Jinx don't hear him. "Little caterpillar!" they shout.

"Shhhh . . ." says Jess, worriedly. He doesn't want Willow to hear them and find out what kind of animal Chloe is.

Read alone

The puppies jump up at the tree and shout for Chloe, but they can't see her.

Read aloud   Read along

Just then, Willow appears. "Hi, Jess," she calls. "Can I meet Chloe now?"

"Er . . . no, Willow," says Jess, going over to meet her. "I think Chloe's still . . . sleeping!"

"Oh well, that gives me more time to guess what kind of animal she is," replies Willow. "Give me a clue. Is she big or small?"

"Small," answers Jess.

"A bird?" guesses Willow.

"No," says Jess, happily. "You'll find out soon. I'll get you when she's . . . woken up. Bye!"

Willow asks if she can meet Chloe now.
Jess says that she's sleeping.

Read alone

Read aloud   Read along

"We've got to find Chloe before Willow guesses what animal she is," says Jess.

Jess and the puppies go back to the tree. Billie and Baa come to find out what all the noise is about.

"We are trying to find Chloe the caterpillar," explains Jess. "Billie, can you climb up into the leaves to look for her?"

"You bet I can! Here I go!" replies Billie, and she jumps out of Baa's hat and scurries up the tree.

Read alone

Billie climbs up the Twisty Tree to look for Chloe in the leaves.

Read aloud Read along

Billie disappears among the leaves.
Then she shouts, "Wow, I've found
something! It's a red bug with black spots!"

"Is it a ladybird? A worm? An ant?" asks Jess.

What animal do you think Billie has found?

"That's a ladybird, Billie!"
says Jess. "But we're looking
for a caterpillar."

"Sorry, Jess. She's not up here!" says Billie
and she comes down from the tree.

Read alone

Billie finds a ladybird, but she can't find Chloe the caterpillar.

Read aloud   Read along

The puppies go off to play chase. But Billie and Baa are going to help Jess.

"What do you think has happened to Chloe the caterpillar?" asks Jess.

"Maybe she's tired of eating leaves," says Billie.

"I once saw a caterpillar eating an apple," says Baa.

"Good thinking, Baa!" says Jess. "Come on, let's go to the orchard."

Billie looks at all the apples in the orchard, but she can't find Chloe the caterpillar.

Read alone

The friends look in the orchard, but Chloe isn't there.

Read aloud   Read along

Just then, Horace hops over to join them. "Jess, I found this on the blackcurrant bush," he says.

"That looks like Chloe's coat!" gasps Jess. "But where's Chloe?"

"Caterpillars shed their skins," says Horace.

"You mean Chloe might look a little bit different now?" asks Jess.

"Yes, Jess," replies Horace. "So I think we should look for Chloe by the pond again. But this time, we'll need Detective Billie's help!"

Read alone

Horace finds Chloe's coat. They decide to look by the pond again.

At the pond, Billie looks in the blackcurrant bush as Jess, Horace and Baa peek through the leaves.

"Wow!" says Billie, rustling in the leaves. "Look, Jess! What do you think this is?"

"I don't know," says Jess. "But it's kind of Chloe-shaped!"

"Maybe it's her house!" says Billie.

"Look!" says Jess. "It's moving!"

Read alone

Billie finds something like Chloe in the leaves. It starts to move!

Read aloud

Read along

Then a butterfly opens
its wings and flies out from the
blackcurrant bush.

Jess, Billie and Baa gasp, "Wow! It's amazing!"

"It's not Chloe though," says Jess.
"It's a butterfly!"

Just then, Willow joins them at Horace's pond.
"So this is Chloe!" she says. "I'd never have
guessed she was a butterfly!"

Billie and Baa get confused. They thought
Chloe was a caterpillar.

Read alone

A butterfly flies out of the leaves!
The friends are very surprised.

Read aloud   Read along

Willow is admiring the butterfly. "She's absolutely beautiful, Jess," she says.

"Er, Willow . . . that's not Chloe," says Jess. "Chloe's a caterpillar."

"Not any more she isn't, Jess," says Willow.

"What?" asks Jess.

"Caterpillars turn into butterflies," says Willow.

"They do?" asks Jess.

Read alone

Willow tells the friends that caterpillars turn into butterflies.

Billie and Baa are even more confused!
"Huh? What?" they say.

"A butterfly lays an egg," says Willow.
"The egg hatches into a caterpillar . . ."

"And then the caterpillar grows up and sheds
its coat, like we found!" says Horace.

"That's right! Then it makes itself a cocoon, just
like you saw," says Willow. "And after about ten
days, the caterpillar has turned into a butterfly!"

"And out it comes!" says Jess, happily.

Read alone

"A caterpillar loses its coat and turns into a butterfly," says Willow.

Read aloud   Read along

"Now we know what's happened to Chloe the caterpillar," says Jess. "Yippety Yay! Yippety yay! Yippety yay!"

"Hurray!" cry his friends.

"Chloe the caterpillar turned into a butterfly!" giggles Jess, and Chloe lands on Jess' head and crawls down his nose!

Read alone

"Chloe the caterpillar turned into a butterfly!" says Jess.

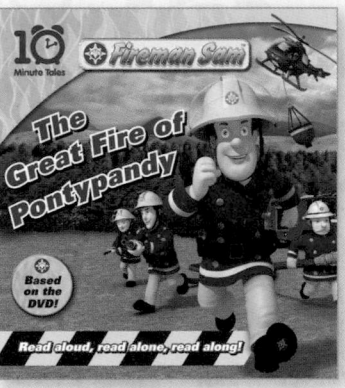

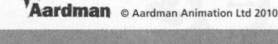